Livin' the Life

JESSIE

Livin' the Life

Adapted by Lexi Ryals

Based on the series created by Pamela Eells O'Connell

Part One is based on the episode "Somebunny's in Trouble," written by Pamela Eells O'Connell

Part Two is based on the episode "Teacher's Pest," written by Sally Lapiduss & Erin Dunlap

Disney PRESS

New York • Los Angeles

Printed in the United States of America

First Edition

1 3 5 7 9 10 8 6 4 2

V475-2873-0-14157

Library of Congress Control Number: 2014936662

ISBN 978-1-4231-8411-9

For more Disney Press fun, visit www.disneybooks.com

Visit DisneyChannel.com

SUSTAINABLE FORESTRY INITIATIVE

Certified Chain of Custody
Promoting Sustainable Forestry

www.sfiprogram.org
SFI-01054

The SFI label applies to the text stock

Part 1

Dear Diary,

Everything has been going really well lately. Emma and Ravi have been spending more time together. Luke has been so invested in sports he's been keeping out of trouble . . . for now.

   For the past few days I've been pretty busy with Zuri. After school, it takes every ounce of my energy to get her to stop talking about how much she wishes she could take home the pet bunny from her classroom. The girl won't give up! At least her class pet isn't a snake or something else scaly. . . . Between our lizard and whatever's growing in Luke's room, we already have enough crusty things living in this penthouse!

Jessie

Chapter 1

After school had let out for the day one crisp, breezy autumn afternoon, Jessie and Zuri strolled into the lobby of their apartment building. Glancing at Zuri's huge purple backpack, Jessie cringed, thinking that Zuri already had enough homework to last the two of them till December. Before Jessie and Zuri entered the elevator, Zuri stopped walking.

"Jessie," she said, "can I volunteer to bring Lucy, our class bunny rabbit, home for the weekend?"

"Zuri, when it comes to responsibility, you

don't have a great track record," said Jessie. "Remember when you promised to start flossing regularly?"

"I floss my teeth!" Zuri retorted, putting down her backpack to point at her pearly whites.

"Really?" said Jessie, wrinkling her nose. "At your last cleaning, there was so much plaque the dentist fainted."

A smile broke across Zuri's face as she looked dreamily into the distance. "He went down like a submarine," she said.

Suddenly, Zuri's backpack began hopping across the floor.

"Wow," said Jessie, pointing at it. "That is some hyperactive homework!" She walked over and kneeled down to open the backpack. Inside was a white bunny rabbit with a few black spots.

"Hmm, that's interesting," said Jessie, scooping

up the bunny. "I don't remember packing you a *bunny* for lunch!" She stood up and saw that Zuri looked squeamish.

"I might have already volunteered. Oops," Zuri said nervously, recoiling.

"Zuri, the sewers are overflowing with all the fish you forgot to feed." Jessie covered the bunny's ears. "*And I don't think we can flush a bunny!*" she whispered.

"That won't happen this time. I promise!" said Zuri, clasping her hands together. "Please, please, please?" She tilted her head and opened her eyes pleadingly.

"Wow," said Jessie. "Three pleases, the puppy dog eyes, and a head tilt." She spoke into the bunny's ear. "The begging trifecta!"

Zuri continued to pout.

"I don't stand a chance, do I?" Jessie asked her.

"Nope," said Zuri. "Give in or I'll close with the lip quiver." Her bottom lip trembled. "And a single tear," she said.

"Fine. I give," said Jessie, handing the bunny to Zuri.

Zuri smiled.

Jessie put her hands on her hips. "Next time I negotiate with you, I'm wearing a blindfold and headphones."

Zuri giggled as Jessie patted the bunny playfully on the head.

❤ ❤ ❤

It was a warm autumn day in Central Park. Emma snuggled down into her new white faux-fur jacket and sighed happily. She loved autumn. It meant two of her favorite things at once—fresh fall fashions and cute Walden Academy boys playing flag football in the park. She and Ravi had stopped and sat on a bench to watch a flag football game on their way home, and she was hoping to catch a glimpse of her current crush.

"See, I like flag football because it lacks the physical contact that makes traditional football so perilous," Ravi told her as they watched the boys kick off.

"So you want to play with them?" Emma asked.

Ravi laughed. "Oh, dear gods, no!" he said.

Emma stood up and pointed out the quarterback, who was busy lining up his play. "That's Brett Summers," Emma told Ravi. "Isn't he dreamy? I am *so* crushing on him."

Just then, Brett came toward them to catch a pass and ran straight into Emma. She fell to the ground and he landed right on top of her.

"And now *he* is crushing on *you*," Ravi told her.

Brett stood up quickly and reached down to

help Emma up. "Sorry, my bad. You okay, Emma?" he asked.

"Sure. . . . Spleens are overrated," Emma said, brushing off her jacket and then quickly batting her eyelashes and smiling at Brett. "Anyway, great catch!"

"So, you like football?" he asked.

"Love it!" Emma chirped brightly. "It's my third-favorite thing that involves feet." She looked into the distance, then back at Brett. "After shoes and pedicures!"

Brett chuckled. "So, are you a Jets fan?"

"Duh!" Emma answered. "Especially taking a private one to the Riviera."

"Ha! You're funny," Brett said.

Emma looked around, confused. She hadn't meant to be funny. "Yes," she said slowly. "Yes, I am?"

"Do you . . . want to watch the game with me tomorrow?" Brett asked.

"Oh! Game!" Emma exclaimed. "Sure! Let's watch it in my screening room. We have a seventy-five-inch screen and free popcorn!"

"Sold!" Brett flashed her a wide smile. "And I promise not to use you as a tackling dummy." He shot Emma a smoldering gaze. "Even if you are the prettiest one I've ever clobbered." He reached down, grabbed the football, and then headed back into the game.

Emma giggled and skipped over to Ravi. "He thinks I'm pretty!"

"Compared to a *tackling dummy*," Ravi pointed out. "Emma, you know less about sports than I do. And I thought the *Super* Bowl was what Bertram ate *soup* out of."

"I can fake it," she said confidently. "I mean,

this jacket is faux fur, but it looks real. All I have to do is *look* like a football fan for an afternoon. How hard can it be?"

Just then, the football flew through the air toward them again.

"Incoming!" Ravi yelled, and they both ran.

❤ ❤ ❤

That night, Jessie gathered Emma, Luke, Ravi, and Zuri for dinner in the kitchen. As Bertram passed out dinner rolls for their pasta dishes, Zuri said, "Guess what, everyone. I'm taking care of the class bunny this weekend!"

"Bunny?" Bertram's eyes grew wide and he stepped away from the table. "There's a bunny in the house?" he asked, clearly panicked. He placed down the bread basket.

"Why do I feel like the crazy train is about to pull into Bertramville?" Luke said, shaking his head.

"I happen to have an *intense* rabbit phobia!" Bertram said defensively.

"All aboard!" Jessie muttered under her breath.

"Once my mommy took me to the mall to see the Easter Bunny," Bertram explained, recalling the painful memory. "I sat on his moth-eaten suit and stared into his red, glowing eyes. Then he made that horrible bunny face!" Bertram contorted his face so that he resembled a bunny, with only his two front teeth showing. He snorted and pretended to chomp on an invisible carrot. "Long story short, I wet myself. . . ." His voice cracked. "And the Easter Bunny."

"Poor Bertram. How old were you?" Ravi asked sympathetically.

Bertram cleared his throat. "Fourteen," he replied.

Ravi grimaced. Luke tried not to laugh.

"Bertram, there's nothing to be afraid of!" Zuri pulled Lucy out from under the table and held her up. "See?"

Bertram screamed, hopped backward, and ran out of the kitchen.

"And the crazy train has left the station," Jessie said, rolling her eyes.

"Can we please give Bertram the day off so he doesn't embarrass me in front of Brett when we watch the game?" Emma begged Jessie.

Luke snorted. "Considering you think a quarterback is the guy who makes change for the team, Bertram's pee stories are the *least* of your problems."

"Hey, if you need advice about sports, just ask Luke," Jessie told Emma. "It may be the only time he can give you anything . . . besides lice."

At that, Luke, who had been scratching his head, stopped.

"Luke, would you mind helping me learn about sports?" Emma asked in a supersweet voice.

Luke raised an eyebrow. He wasn't buying her whole nice act. "Let's see. . . . From now on, would you mind calling me Lord Master of Awesomeness?"

"How about I stop calling you Vomit Bag and do your chores for three days?" Emma countered, all the sweetness gone from her voice.

"Deal," Luke said, looking pleased with himself.

"Hold the phone!" said Zuri. "*We* have *chores*?"

Dear Diary,

So Emma has a date with a cute flag football jock, which is just great for her! The only guy on the football team who ever asked me out was the water boy, and he made *me* bring *him* the water. ~~Hopefully~~ she'll be able to learn enough from Luke to make it through one football game without blowing her cover. I'll have to remind her that the line of scrimmage isn't a new line of makeup.

Jessie

Chapter 2

The next morning, Jessie walked onto the terrace to find Ravi staring through a cage at Lucy. "Hey, Ravi, whatcha doin'?" Jessie asked.

Ravi scrunched up his nose as he studied the bunny. "Failing to understand what you people find so cute about this creature. It has no claws! No fangs! No *thirst* for *blood*..."

"Ravi, you may find this hard to believe, but most people prefer their pets *not* to be flesh-eating monsters," Jessie explained.

"I guess it takes all kinds," Ravi said, shrugging.

Jessie peered through Lucy's cage at her food dish. It was empty. Jessie sighed, exasperated. "You see? This is exactly what I was afraid of! Zuri didn't fill up Lucy's food dish." Jessie opened the cage door, took the dish, and walked to the bag of rabbit food across the terrace. She scooped the food into the dish and grabbed a carrot.

"Zuri was irresponsible?" said Ravi with feigned surprise. "In other news, the sun rose this morning!" he said sarcastically as he headed inside the penthouse.

"Seriously, how hard is it to take care of one little bunny?" Jessie muttered to herself, heading back toward the cage. She nearly dropped the dish when she saw the open cage door and no Lucy. "Uh-oh," she groaned. "Apparently pretty hard!"

Frantic, Jessie ran into the penthouse to search for Lucy.

Ravi looked up from the couch, startled, as she burst into the living room.

"Ravi," Jessie said, "something totally horrible has happened!" She looked across the floor, under the table, and beneath the pillows on the couch, but there was no sign of the rabbit.

"THE EARTH SLIPPED FROM ITS AXIS AND WE ARE HURTLING TOWARD COSMIC DOOM!?" Ravi screamed, looking terrified and covering his ears with his hands.

"Worse—I lost a bunny!" Jessie answered, ripping a pillow from the couch and accidentally throwing it at him.

"Hey, watch it!" Ravi yelped. "I am the only small adorable creature you have not lost yet!"

"Help me!" Jessie whispered, looking frazzled. "I can't believe she's gone!"

Just then, Bertram came in carrying a full

laundry basket. "Who's gone?" he asked, looking excited. "One of the girls? Did Christina finally take my suggestion about boarding school?" He smiled, pressed his hands together, and looked at them dreamily.

Jessie started pulling clothes out of Bertram's basket and throwing them over her shoulder. "Lucy escaped!" she explained.

Bertram dropped the basket on the ground as though it were full of, well, bunnies. "You mean there's a bloodthirsty, savage rodent running around the apartment?" he asked, alarmed.

"No. I mean there's a cute, snuggly bunny running around the apartment!" Jessie said, correcting him.

"Po-tay-toe, po-tah-toe. It's all fun and games until someone gets nuzzled to death in their sleep!" Bertram hurried out of the living room, wailing in a fit of fear.

❤ ❤ ❤

Emma held out the bucket of gourmet popcorn to Brett. He was seated next to her in the screening room, watching the Jets game and wearing his Walden Academy flag football jersey. He looked so cute that she was having trouble even remembering that the game was on.

"So, Emma, do you think the Jets will make the playoffs?" Brett asked as he took a handful of popcorn.

"Good question," she said overly loudly, turning toward the back of the room slightly. *"Do I think the Jets will make the playoffs?"*

Luke, hiding behind the back row of seats, heard the question and texted Emma an answer as quickly as he could.

Emma's phone buzzed. She checked it and then turned to Brett confidently. "Not if their quarterback can't figure out how to beat a zone blimp."

Brett looked at her quizzically. "You mean 'blitz'?"

"I do?" Emma laughed nervously. "I mean, of course I do! More popcorn?"

"Stupid autocorrect," Luke muttered to himself.

"So, who do you think will make the playoffs?" Brett asked as the game switched to a commercial.

Emma's phone buzzed again. "Oh!" She read the text and then answered. "Definitely the Green Bay Porkers!"

"Packers!" Luke moaned to himself more loudly than he realized. "Dang this phone!"

Brett looked at Emma, confused. "Who's that?" he asked, standing.

She shrugged and also stood up.

He walked to the back of the room and peered behind the seats to find Luke crouched on the floor. Luke stood up and waved.

"Oh, hey, Brett," Luke said sheepishly, looking around for an excuse. "I was just, uh, looking for my . . . old raisin." He picked up a small brown ball from the floor and popped it into his mouth. "Not a raisin." He choked, gagging a little. "Lucy's got some 'splaining to do."

"Luke?" Brett asked. "What's going on?" He looked from Luke to Emma.

"Yeah, Luke, what is going on?" Emma asked, her eyes wide as she tried to silently urge Luke to cover for her.

"Really, Emma?" Luke scowled. "You want to play *that* game?"

"Oh, okay." Emma sighed and then turned to Brett. "Brett, the truth is . . . I wanted you to like me, so I pretended to know a lot about sports. But I don't know anything about sports, so I asked Luke to tell me what to say."

"I can't believe you did that!" Brett exclaimed, taken aback. Then he smiled. "That's so cool! No girl's ever done something that nice for me before."

Emma smiled back.

Just then, the crowd on the TV erupted into a cheer.

"Touchdown! Jets!" Luke yelled, jumping between Emma and Brett.

Brett turned toward the TV and his face fell. "Aw, man, I missed it!"

"Upper deck, bro!" Luke said, reaching up and high-fiving Brett.

"Dude, you gotta stay and watch the rest of the game with us," Brett insisted.

"Sweet, I'm in!" Luke plopped down into Emma's seat next to Brett.

Emma scowled at him. "Luke, don't you think you're being a little rude?"

"Right, where are my manners?" Luke said. He turned to Brett. "Brett, would you like anything to drink?"

"I could go for a root beer," Brett replied.

"Good idea!" Luke said. "Emma, two root beers."

Emma rolled her eyes and headed for the kitchen. Her date was not going as planned, but at least Brett still liked her, even if she wasn't as sports savvy as Luke.

Dear Diary,

Well, Emma came clean to Brett and it turned out that he likes her even though she doesn't know a thing about sports! There's no point in pretending to be someone you aren't just to get a guy to like you. I'm so proud of her! Who I'm *not* proud of is *me*! I can't believe I lost Lucy. I'm hoping I can find her before Zuri realizes she's missing. Otherwise I may go missing mysteriously, too! Zuri does NOT mess around. *Gulp.*

Jessie

Chapter 3

Jessie had turned the penthouse upside down looking for Lucy, and she was checking the living room again.

"She has to be here somewhere!" Jessie muttered. Then she called softly, "Here, Lucy! Lucy? Who's a good bunny?"

The piano lid popped open and Ravi pulled himself partially out, waving a carrot around. "Well, Lucy is not in here," he announced.

"Jessie!" Zuri called from the other room.

Frantic, Jessie pushed Ravi back into the piano

and slammed the lid, accidentally smashing Ravi's fingers.

"Ahhhh!" Ravi screamed, his yelp muffled by the piano lid.

Zuri sprinted into the room.

Jessie leaned casually against the piano, trying to look like she hadn't spent the morning on a wild rabbit chase. "Hey, Zuri," Jessie said sweetly.

"Have you seen Lucy?" Zuri asked.

Jessie threw up her hands, laughing. "I can't keep track of all your little friends!"

"You know Lucy!" Zuri insisted. "Short . . . furry . . . poops on the floor?"

"Hmmm. Could you be more specific?" Jessie said, looking thoughtful.

"I must've left the cage open and she escaped! I am so irresponsible," Zuri said, looking crest-fallen.

Jessie exhaled loudly. She couldn't let Zuri blame herself, as tempting as it was. "No, no. You didn't lose Lucy. You're doing a great job," Jessie said, trying to encourage Zuri and think of a cover story. "You didn't lose Lucy. I . . . took Lucy to . . . the bunny groomers."

"Why? She wasn't dirty."

"True. But . . . I had a coupon . . . which was about to expire," Jessie said, and sat down at the piano. "Yes. That's it. Now, if you'll excuse me, I feel like playing the piano." She banged at the keys halfheartedly, making a horrible racket.

"What you need is a coupon for piano lessons," Zuri said under her breath, and she went up to her room.

As soon as Zuri was out of sight, Jessie stood and opened the lid of the piano again. Ravi pulled himself up, rubbing his hand and looking slightly cross-eyed. "Not cool, Jessie," he moaned. "Not cool."

❤   ❤   ❤

The next day, Emma and Brett had another date, but this time Emma had planned it. She had plates of snacks and her favorite board game, Chick Chat, all spread out on the table in the living room for when Brett arrived. After he arrived—looking oh so cute—they sat on the couch to play.

"Brett, are you sure you don't mind playing a board game instead of watching football?" Emma asked him.

"Nah. I mean, you went to all the trouble to learn about sports for me," Brett said, smiling at her.

Emma smiled back. "Well, that's what couples do." She just loved the idea of Brett being her new boyfriend.

"Right. And I'm sure I'll love playing . . ." Brett looked at the game box and read the name off the top. "Chick Chat."

"It's my favorite!" Emma exclaimed. "You get to share secrets, earn good-hair-day points, and everybody wins! So really it's a lot like football."

"Right," Brett said slowly, his eyes looking a little glazed. "Only without the sports . . . or fun."

Just then, Brett's phone beeped with a text message. He read it and laughed out loud, tilting back his head, before typing a quick reply.

"Who's that?" Emma asked.

"Uh, no one," Brett said quickly, putting down the phone. "Can I go first?"

He rolled the dice and moved his game piece forward six spaces on the board.

"Oh, no! You landed on a Nothing-to-Wear Square!" Emma told him. "Now you have to go back two spaces and buy a date outfit."

"You mean like . . . new sneakers?" Brett asked.

Emma gasped. "Sneakers on a date? Ew. I'm going to pretend you didn't say that."

Brett cringed. "Sorry. I guess I'm better at games where I get to hit or tackle someone."

Emma thought for a moment and then said brightly, "Well, if you draw a Hissy Fit Card, you get to slap the person to your left!"

Brett's phone beeped again. It was another text. He read it, smiled, and then made an effort to look serious. "Hey, sorry, Emma, but I've actually gotta split. I have to, uh, study," he told her.

"But I thought we were going to go see that rom-com, *The Really Attractive Woman Who's Single for No Reason*?" Emma protested.

"I would love to, but my studies come first. You know how much athletes care about education,"

Brett insisted. "Can't you go see the movie with one of your friends?"

"I guess so . . ." Emma began, but Brett stood and took his empty snack plate into the kitchen.

Suspicious, Emma picked up his phone from the couch and scrolled through his texts. "He deleted his texts?" she muttered to herself. "Why would he do that? Something's going on." She reached over and checked Brett's jacket pockets. Bingo! She found a slip of paper with a phone number written on it. Narrowing her eyes, she stuffed the paper into her own pocket just as he came back into the room, and she smiled at him.

"Here's your jacket, which has an unbelievable amount of pockets, by the way," she said, holding it out for him. "Have fun studying!"

"What?" Brett asked, looking confused as he slipped into his jacket. "Oh, right. Learning rocks!

Have fun at your movie!" He smiled and then got on the elevator. As soon as the doors closed, Emma's smile vanished.

Jessie came rushing down the stairs, but she immediately stopped when she saw the sad look on Emma's face.

"What's wrong?" Jessie asked gently. "Did you land on a Nothing-to-Wear Square?"

"No! I think Brett might be *cheating* on me!" Emma explained. "Look. I found this phone number in his pocket. I bet it's from a girl!" She showed the paper to Jessie.

"Emma, do not jump to conclusions. I once thought my boyfriend was cheating on me because he always smelled like perfume and had lipstick on his collar," Jessie told her.

"And was he?" Emma asked.

"Yes." Jessie shook her head. "You know what,

that was a bad example. Anyway, does it make you feel better?"

"Well, it certainly makes me feel worse for you," Emma admitted.

"Don't you move, you little rodent," Jessie growled.

"Whoa! Back off, old lady!" Emma countered, taking a step back.

"Not you!" Jessie shushed her. "Look." She pointed across the room, where Lucy was hopping through the screening room door. "I told you not to move! No one in this house listens to me!"

Jessie ran toward the curtains and dove after Lucy, crashing to the floor. But when she lifted her hands, there was no Lucy beneath them. "One rabbit's foot may be lucky, but four of them are kicking my butt!" Jessie groaned.

Dear Diary,

Well, I thought Emma's problem was solved, but now she thinks her football cutie is cheating on her. And I still haven't found Lucy. So instead of relaxing and eating my body weight in deep-fried chocolate chip cookies, I've spent all my time searching for a bunny on the lam. Remind me why I took this job again?

Jessie

Chapter 4

Bertram had been in the kitchen for hours making his famous five-spice chili. As he stirred the pot, he sang loudly his own words to the tune of "The Ride of the Valkyries."

"My chili is perfect! Never is runny! Just needs red pepper!" Then he opened the cabinet and came face-to-face with Lucy. "Eek, it's a bunny!"

Lucy leapt from the cabinet right onto Bertram's chest. "Aaaaaaarghhh!" Bertram screamed. He fell backward behind the island as he tried to get Lucy off him.

Hearing his scream, Jessie ran in. "You found Lucy?" she asked.

Bertram pulled himself up from behind the island, with no bunny in sight. "She attacked me!" he said breathlessly. "I managed to fight her off and she went up the back stairs. I think I was nibbled pretty bad."

Jessie patted him on the back reassuringly. "Bertram, I'd help you find a support group . . . but I'm pretty sure no one else on Earth has this problem." Then she dashed up the back stairs to find Lucy.

Bertram looked around nervously and then backed into the living room. The elevator dinged and Bertram, jumpy, spun around. Emma stepped off, looking downcast.

"Emma?" Bertram put his hand to his chest, relieved she wasn't Lucy. He walked over to her.

"I thought you went to some chick flick."

"I did, but I left early," Emma said sadly. "I don't want to watch some girl get the guy when I'm losing mine." Then she grabbed Bertram's collar and shouted, "Brett's cheating on me!"

"Oh, that's terrible! And after you gave him the best forty-eight hours of your life," Bertram said with mock sympathy. "I think you should have a night on the town anyway."

Emma nodded. "Because I shouldn't let some silly boy get me down?"

Bertram snorted. "Because it means more chili for me."

"You're right. I'm not going to just sit here and be upset. I'm going to call up this other woman and find out who she is." Emma took out her phone and the slip of paper she'd found in Brett's jacket. A determined expression crossed her face.

"Again, only interested in your problem inasmuch as it pertains to chili," Bertram reminded her.

Emma punched in the number as Bertram walked hesitantly back toward the kitchen, his eyes watching the floor for any sign of the rogue bunny.

A gurgling noise caught their attention. Then they heard it again and again.

Bertram turned back to Emma, looking offended. "That's rude. My chili happens to be delicious."

Emma put up her hand. "That wasn't me. Wait a minute. . . ." She followed the noise into the screening room, where she found Luke and Brett watching football. Luke answered his phone, which was programmed with a gurgling ringtone.

"Hey, Emma," Luke said into his phone,

motioning Brett to be quiet so Emma wouldn't hear him. "How's the movie?"

"Well," Emma said into her phone while standing in the doorway. "There's a lot more heartbreak and betrayal than I was expecting!"

Luke and Brett both froze at the sound of her voice and then turned toward the door. Emma was giving them both a look that could kill. Brett jumped up and rushed to her. "Emma, I swear, it's not what it looks like."

"Good," Emma said sarcastically. "Because it looks like my new boyfriend lied to me about having to study so he could watch football with my brother!"

"Well, then I guess it is what it looks like," Luke said, snickering.

Brett turned to Luke. "Dude, FYI, awesome ringtone."

"Thanks, man. You get me," Luke said, and they high-fived.

Emma looked from Luke to Brett and then back to Luke, flabbergasted. "Luke, are you wearing Brett's jersey?" she asked incredulously.

"I got cold," Luke said sheepishly.

Emma was horrified. "Ew," she said.

Dear Diary,

Lucy is still missing. Emma's boyfriend wasn't cheating on her, per se, but he was lying to her to spend time with Luke. Bertram is on the verge of a heart attack. The only thing going my way is the fact that Zuri had a day packed with playdates and won't be home for a little while longer. I still might have time to turn things around. . . . Too bad I don't have a lucky rabbit's foot—or better yet, a whole rabbit, safe and sound in her cage!

Jessie

Chapter 5

Jessie was turning over the couch cushions for the fifth time, looking for Lucy.

"Lucy! Lucy!?" Jessie called. "Where are you, you stupid rabbit?"

She found a five-dollar bill wedged in the bottom of the couch and smiled to herself. She looked around and, seeing no one, slipped it into her pocket. "Lucy!"

"Jessie!" Ravi called as he walked down the stairs.

"Ahh! Ravi," Jessie said nervously. "How

long have you been standing there?"

"Do not worry," Ravi assured her. "I did not see you put that five-dollar bill in your pocket. But I have dire news. . . ."

"It can wait," Jessie said. "We have to find Lucy!"

Ravi grimaced. "I am afraid Mrs. Kipling beat us to it. I found what was left of her in Mrs. Kipling's cage." He held out a piece of fluffy white fur.

Jessie grabbed it from him and moaned. "Nooooooo!"

Just then, Zuri walked off the elevator, home from her last playdate of the day. She rushed over to a distraught Jessie and Ravi.

"Jessie, what's the matter?" Zuri asked.

"Um . . ." Jessie covered. "It just occurred to me that I . . . should've gone to college."

Zuri narrowed her eyes. "What's that ball of fluff you've got in your hand?" she asked suspiciously.

"Ravi's belly button lint," Jessie lied.

"I have a very deep innie," Ravi said, playing along.

"Oh, okay." Zuri shrugged and went up to her room.

Ravi and Jessie exchanged looks.

"I can't believe she bought it," Jessie said.

"We were saved by the fact that only Mrs. Kipling has seen me topless," Ravi replied.

"I also can't believe Mrs. Kipling ate Lucy for lunch!" Jessie added, studying the tuft of fur.

"Technically, it was more teatime."

"Who cares what time it was?" Jessie snapped. "The point is Zuri's class pet is halfway down a giant lizard's colon!"

"Technically, it would only be in her—" Ravi began, but Jessie interrupted.

"Correct me again at your own risk!" she warned him.

"Got it," Ravi said. Then he added under his breath, "Stomach."

"What am I going to do?" Jessie wailed. "I gave Zuri this big speech about being responsible. And now, because of me, Lucy hippity-hopped into the light."

"Here is a wacky idea. You could tell Zuri the truth!" Ravi suggested.

"I can't do that!"

"Because it will break her heart?"

"Because she'll break my legs!" Jessie countered. "Remember what Zuri did to that kid in the park who lost her doll?"

Ravi winced. "Yes, I have never seen someone

get picked up by their nostrils before."

"It was a snot-filled horror," Jessie said, shaking her head. Then she perked up. "Wait! I have an idea."

"I cannot wait to hear your great idea," Ravi said encouragingly.

"All I need are some cotton balls, animal-safe dye, and a new rabbit!" Jessie beamed at him.

Ravi sighed. "I continue to wait."

❤ ❤ ❤

Back in the screening room, Emma was at her wit's end. She just couldn't believe that Brett would lie to her so he could hang out with her gross younger brother instead of enjoying a romantic afternoon with her. What was *wrong* with him?

"Brett, if you wanted to watch the game with Luke, why didn't you just tell me?" Emma asked him.

"I didn't want to hurt your feelings," Brett explained.

"Well, it's too late for that!" Emma stomped her foot.

Luke tried to butt in. "Emma, I really think—"

"And you, Luke!" Emma cut him off. "I can't believe you did this to me. We're family!"

"Don't blame him," Brett said. He took her hand. "I knew you wanted to see that movie, but I really wanted to watch the game with Luke. It's my fault. I was weak! So weak . . ."

Emma turned away dramatically. "I just can't look at you right now."

"Enough! This is all my fault!" Luke interjected.

Brett turned to Luke and put his hand on Luke's shoulder. "No, Luke. Don't blame yourself!"

"Please, Brett, I feel cheap enough as it is." Luke hung his head. "I'm sorry, Emma."

Emma threw a hand up in the air. She looked like she was going to cry.

"There's only one thing to do. Brett . . ." Luke continued. He couldn't stand to see his sister so unhappy. "I don't think we should see each other anymore. Have I cherished our time together? Yes. But it's over."

"Luke, no!" Brett looked horrified.

"We'll always have the Jets games," Luke said wistfully.

"Luke, don't be rash!" Brett pleaded.

Luke took off Brett's jersey and gave it back to him. "I said it's over!"

Brett nodded and started to walk out, but he stopped just shy of the door.

"No! Don't look back," Luke begged him.

Brett took a deep breath and walked out without turning around.

Emma looked from the door to Luke and shook her head. "What the heck just happened here?"

Luke cringed. "I made a mistake. I never should have come between you and your boyfriend. Can you forgive me?"

Emma sighed. "I guess so. The truth is . . . Brett and I really don't have that much in common. And I think he was only pretending to like Chick Chat."

"Emma . . . are you saying what I think you're saying?" Luke asked hopefully.

Emma nodded and grinned. "Yeah, I'm going to break up with him. He's all yours."

"Yes!" Luke exclaimed, and then hugged his sister. "Thank you, thank you, thank you!" He hugged her again and then ran after Brett. "Brett! Come back! The Rangers game is on in twenty minutes!"

Emma plopped down in a chair and grabbed the remote. "Ugh! I am done with boys." Then she leaned forward to get a better look at the football players on TV and brightened. "Oooh. He's cute!"

Ravi looked skeptically at the wiggling imposter bunny he held. Jessie was dabbing at the rabbit with a cotton ball dipped in black dye. She was creating dark spots on the rabbit to make it look just like Lucy. Jessie hoped her plan was going to work.

"Okay, this is going to work," Jessie announced confidently.

"How can you be sure?" Ravi asked.

"'Cause I got nothing else." She pulled out a picture of Lucy and compared it to the new rabbit. "There! They could be twins. Zuri will never know the difference."

Zuri walked out onto the terrace, looking

excited when she thought she saw Lucy through the door. Jessie threw the bowl of dye and cotton balls into a planter nearby before Zuri could see them.

After a quick glance at the bunny, Zuri turned to Jessie with a stern look on her face. "Hey, what happened to Lucy?" Zuri asked.

"Guard your nostrils," Ravi hissed at Jessie.

"Zuri, what do you mean? Nothing happened to good old Lucy! Which is this little gal right here . . . Lucy . . . the bunny . . ."

Ravi passed the bunny to Zuri.

Zuri took the rabbit and studied it for a moment. "She looks different. And her nose is twitching a lot slower."

"No, it's not," Jessie countered. She reached over and pushed the bunny's nose up and down faster with her finger.

"Jessie, why are you twitching her nose?" Zuri asked.

"It's a little game we play, see?" Jessie said, her voice getting more and more shrill with anxiety. Then she reached over and twitched Ravi's nose for him.

"Fun!" Ravi said nasally.

"Okay," Zuri said, looking skeptically at them both. "I think Lucy and I will just head upstairs. And not because you're freaking me out at all," she added sarcastically. She cuddled the bunny to her chest and carried it up to her room.

"You can stop playing with my nose now," Ravi suggested in the same nasal tone.

"Oh, sorry!" Jessie let go. Then she smiled gleefully. "I told you she'd believe that's her bunny!"

Dear Diary,

Well, it looks like I'm in the clear.

Emma dumped Brett, but she doesn't

seem upset about it. And, silver lining,

Luke got a new BFF out of this whole

debacle. I think they'll be very happy

together. And Zuri is snuggling with a

bunny named Lucy. We'll just never tell

her that that rabbit is really Lucy 2.0.

As long as Mrs. Kipling doesn't burp

up any more fur, she'll never find out

the truth! Time to go rub Mrs. Kipling's

tummy!

Jessie

Chapter 6

Later that night, in the living room, Jessie and Ravi were stretched out on the couch, watching TV. Jessie was feeling inspired, by Emma, to watch a rom-com, and who better to watch it with than her partner in crime?

"This is not my bunny!" Zuri announced from the staircase. Her shirt was covered in black dye and she was waving a streaky-coated Lucy 2.0 in Jessie's and Ravi's faces.

"What makes you think that?" Jessie asked nervously.

"Her spots are coming off, and she smells like Mom after a hair appointment," Zuri told her.

"Because . . . I gave Lucy some lowlights," Jessie said, covering. "It really minimizes those ears."

"Not your best," Ravi hissed at Jessie.

Zuri glared at both of them. "Okay, truth time. Where is Lucy?"

Jessie sighed. She knew that she had to come clean. "Okay . . . the truth is . . . I lost Lucy."

"What!?" Zuri exclaimed. "That better just be the name of an old TV show!"

A scream cut through the penthouse. Everyone ran into the kitchen, where they found Bertram crouched on top of a stool, pointing at the floor and gibbering, "The horror . . . the horror!"

Lucy was sitting on the floor, innocently twitching her cute little nose.

"Lucy!" Zuri said joyfully. "Here, hold this." She

thrust Lucy 2.0 into Bertram's hands. Then she picked up Lucy and cradled the rabbit against her chest.

Bertram held Lucy 2.0 as far away from him as he could and sobbed in terror. Jessie mercifully took the rabbit from him and put it in the cage.

"Bertram, calm yourself, man!" Ravi said, cutting through the sobs. "Even I am embarrassed for you, and I am afraid of safety pins."

Jessie's eyebrows shot up. "Really?" she asked.

"There is nothing safe about them," Ravi told her matter-of-factly.

Bertram pointed at the dumbwaiter. "Look what that monster left in there!"

Jessie opened the dumbwaiter door and gasped. The dumbwaiter was filled with cute, fuzzy baby bunnies—all with black-and-white fur just like Lucy's!

"Wow!" Zuri cooed. "That explains why, no matter how many times I fed her, Lucy's bowl was always empty."

"She was eating for . . . fourteen . . . fifteen . . . sixteen!" Ravi said.

Zuri set Lucy down suddenly. "Yuck . . . Make that seventeen." The bunny was still having babies!

"But the good news is Lucy is not dead after all," Ravi said happily.

"Say what now?" Zuri turned to him.

Ravi smiled sheepishly. "That piece of fluff I found in Mrs. Kipling's cage must have come from Emma's faux-fur jacket! I guess Mrs. Kipling ate it. No one tell Emma."

But Emma had heard everything. "What?" she yelled, storming in. "You let that lizard menace into my closet? And she ate my jacket?"

"Uh-oh, someone drew a Hissy Fit Card," Ravi said, and then ran up the back stairs. "This *innie* is *outtie!*"

Emma followed him. "Ravi, if you don't control that lizard, then I will!"

"Zuri, I'm really sorry I doubted you. Turns out you're the responsible one," Jessie said. Then she picked up a baby bunny and cuddled it.

"Thanks, Jessie. Try to remember that when you go to that meeting with my teacher tomorrow," Zuri said guiltily.

"What meeting?" Jessie asked sternly.

"We'll talk," Zuri said, and then held up some baby bunnies to distract Jessie.

Bertram looked like he might pass out. "Nineteen bunnies! Could this get any worse?"

"Obviously you don't know much about bunnies," Jessie said, laughing.

Luke and Brett had spent the entire day watching football and eating pizza bagels. Luke was pretty sure it was the beginning of a long and beautiful friendship.

"I can't wait for baseball season!" Luke smiled. "My dad has Yankees season tickets."

Brett looked concerned. "Wait! You're a *Yankees* fan?"

"Of course! If you live in New York, you're a Yankees fan," Luke told him.

"Unless you're a Mets fan!" Brett said, disgusted. "Ugh, how do you sleep at night?"

"In my Yankees *jammies*, on my Yankees *sheets*, under my twenty-seven Yankees World Series *pennants*! Which I believe is *twenty-five more* than your team!" Luke countered, his voice getting louder and louder.

"How dare you?" Brett shouted. "This . . . is over!"

"It most certainly is," Luke agreed.

Brett headed toward the kitchen with his plate of pizza bagels.

"And, Brett . . ."

"Yeah, Luke?" Brett stopped and turned around hopefully.

"Leave the snacks," Luke said coldly.

Brett narrowed his eyes. "Gladly." Then he threw his plate down and stormed out.

Luke looked at the spilled pizza bagels for a moment, then shrugged, picked them up off the floor, and ate one as Bertram walked in.

"Bertram, throw out everything Brett touched," Luke ordered.

"Great. So that includes you and Emma," Bertram said gleefully.

"Uh-oh," Luke groaned.

Jessie didn't remember packing Zuri a *bunny* for lunch!

At the sight of Zuri's bunny, Bertram hopped away!

Ravi assured Jessie that Zuri's bunny was *not* in the piano.

Emma was thrilled to play Chick Chat with her
new boyfriend, Brett!

Emma wondered who Brett was texting.

"They could be twins!" said Jessie. "Zuri will never know the difference!"

Zuri suspected something was amiss . . . so Jessie
twitched Ravi's nose!

"Wow!" said Zuri. "Where did all these bunnies come from?"

Ravi announced to Luke that he was moving in
with him!

Luke explained that his bedroom was a rule-free zone!

The old cake in Luke's room had grown fuzz.

"Why does my cape say 'Furtenfurter'?" Jessie asked
Mrs. Falkenberg.

Jessie pretended she was interested in Quidditch.

The truth was that Jessie couldn't stand Quidditch!

For a change of pace, Jessie dressed up as the Golden Snitch!

Jessie decided that Mrs. Falkenberg deserved
a real best friend!

Dear Diary,

I think Zuri's teacher may be in for a shock when she realizes that she now has nineteen class bunny rabbits. Hopefully she won't hold it against Zuri—although Bertram may hold this against all of us forever. Just to be on the safe side, I'm not eating any of that chili he made. The more chili he eats, the happier he'll be!

Jessie

Part 2

Dear Diary,

Well, it's back to school for me this week: I'm volunteering as the teacher's aide for Zuri's class! Zuri has been having a lot of trouble in school this year and I'm determined to figure out what the problem is! (I mean, it can't all be because of Lucy's bunny babies, can it?) She claims her teacher is mean to her. I know Zuri can be a little bit of a handful, but she's not a bad kid—she's just precocious. ~~Hopefully~~ I can help Zuri get on her teacher's good side and then she can coast through the rest of the year. It shouldn't be too difficult, right?

Jessie

Chapter 1

Jessie pounded on Zuri's bedroom door. They had to get a move on or Zuri was going to be late for school.

"Zuri, hurry!" Jessie yelled. "I said 'five minutes' five minutes ago!"

"Oh? You think *my* morning breath is bad?" Ravi said to Mrs. Kipling as he stormed out of his room. "An animal actually *did* die in your mouth!"

Mrs. Kipling followed him out of his room, hissing angrily and whipping her tail back and forth. She slapped Jessie in the legs with her tail as she turned and stormed back into Ravi's room, slamming the door behind her.

"Ow! Only seven-thirty and I already have my first kid-related injury," Jessie groaned, rubbing her calves.

"Mrs. Kipling is being impossible!" Ravi exclaimed.

"You know she always gets cranky just before she sheds her skin," Jessie said.

"But now she is constantly cranky! Ever since the babies hatched, I have been walking on eggshells," Ravi said.

"Well, now that her babies are living in the lizard sanctuary, maybe she has actual empty-nest syndrome."

"Sure, take her side!" Ravi scowled as he turned and headed down the hall. "You women always stick together!"

Mrs. Kipling opened Ravi's door and hissed at him.

"Sisters are doin' it for themselves. Am I right?" Jessie said to her.

Mrs. Kipling nodded and hissed approvingly.

❤ ❤ ❤

Jessie sighed and closed her laptop. She'd gotten the kids off to school and she and Bertram had been having a quiet breakfast, but she couldn't enjoy it.

"Darla just had to e-mail me every detail about the trip she and her boyfriend took to Rio," Jessie grumbled. "The most exotic place Tony's taken me is the Empanada Garden."

Bertram looked at her over the top of his latest issue of *Gentleman's Gentleman Quarterly*. "Hey, nothing says 'I love you' like a deep-fried meat pillow."

A high-pitched laugh echoed through the kitchen. Jessie and Bertram exchanged looks and then both peered at the far wall, from which they thought the sound had come. Jessie walked toward it and opened the dumbwaiter. Zuri was sitting inside, holding two of her dolls. She gave Jessie a sheepish smile.

"Zuri, what are you doing in the dumbwaiter?" Jessie asked. "I put you on the bus!"

"The bus has two doors," Zuri replied. "Now, if you'll excuse me, I'm playing Oprah and Gayle with my dollies." She reached up and started to pull the dumbwaiter door closed, but Jessie stopped her. She pulled Zuri out of the dumb-waiter and led her to the kitchen table.

"Why aren't you in school?" Jessie asked, upset.

"The more important question might be, do my parents know you both just sit around when we're not home?" Zuri asked pointedly.

Bertram held up his hands defensively. "Hey, I am researching kitchen cleaners! Your mother hates it when the stainless steel gets streaky. She can't see herself in the fridge."

"Don't change the subject," Jessie said. "Zuri, why don't you want to go to school?"

"Because," Zuri whined, "Mrs. Falkenberg is the meanest teacher in the world!"

"How could she be mean to you? You're so adorable," Jessie said.

"I know, right?" Zuri nodded. "She's a monster!"

"Zuri, I'm sure you're exaggerating, but tomorrow I start volunteering as your class aide, so I can see what's going on," Jessie said reassuringly.

"So tomorrow I get the house to myself?" Bertram exclaimed, jumping up. "I can play my music as loud as I want! A new Mozart album just dropped, you know."

"You're a wild man, Bertram," Zuri said, shaking her head.

"Yeah, way to let your back hair down," Jessie added, rolling her eyes.

❤ ❤ ❤

The next morning, Jessie walked into Zuri's classroom, ready for her first day as a teacher's aide. She hadn't been so excited since she graduated from high school. She had a brand-new backpack and lunch box and a shiny new name tag.

As soon as Jessie walked in, she spotted Zuri sitting at a desk, looking like a perfect angel. Jessie smiled and waved at Zuri and then headed to Mrs. Falkenberg's desk. Mrs. Falkenberg, her brown hair pulled back in a severe ponytail, was flipping through work sheets.

"Hi, Mrs. Falkenberg. I'm Jessie, your new classroom aide. I brought lunch, a juice box, and safety scissors," Jessie said as an introduction.

"I think Zuri has everything she needs," Mrs. Falkenberg said snidely, raising one eyebrow.

"Oh. Um, they're for me," Jessie said, blushing but still enthusiastic. "So, which is my chair? Can I be near the window? When do I get to mold young minds?"

"No molding," Mrs. Falkenberg snapped. "Just distract them with shiny objects so they don't eat their weight in crayons. Okay?"

"O-kay," Jessie said, feeling intimidated. She could see why Zuri thought her teacher was a little mean.

Mrs. Falkenberg handed a stack of work sheets to Jessie and then sat back in her desk chair. "All right," she said loudly to the class. "While Ms.

Perky Pants here passes out the work sheets, someone tell me a country that borders Germany."

"Why do we need to know where Germany is?"
Zuri asked. "That's the Internet's job."

Mrs. Falkenberg shook her head. "Zuri Ross, I
think we've already had one too many opinions
from you this morning."

Jessie gave Zuri a stern look as she handed her
a work sheet.

Mrs. Falkenberg moved her chair toward the
map. The chair let out a long squeak that sounded
suspiciously like a fart.

"And I think you had one too many burritos
for dinner last night," Zuri retorted, giggling.

All the students in the class laughed loudly.

"It was the chair!" Mrs. Falkenberg exclaimed.
"Zuri Ross, once again, you're first on the Naughty
Board." She jumped up and strode to a whiteboard

with "Naughty List" written at the top in blue marker.

"Not again!" Zuri said.

"Yes again!" Mrs. Falkenberg insisted as she jotted Zuri's name on the board.

Jessie followed the teacher. "I'm so sorry. She's much better behaved at home."

"Jessie, I think we both know that's not true," Zuri whispered to her. "She's mean, but she's not an idiot!"

Dear Diary,

Well, Zuri wasn't wrong. Her teacher, Mrs. Falkenberg, is not a nice lady. She definitely has it in for Zuri. Plus, she's lazy, mean, and she seems to really hate kids. I'm not sure why she even became a teacher to begin with. Still, I'm not giving up—I will make Mrs. Falkenberg like Zuri. Otherwise, Zuri might not make it on to fourth grade!

Jessie

Chapter 2

"So now that you've seen Falkenbooger in action, you get that she's a nightmare, right?" Zuri asked, flopping down next to Jessie on the couch. She had her pj's on and was ready for bed.

"Yeah," Jessie said. "She doesn't seem to be good with kids. Or adults. Even the class bunny was spelling out 'help me' in food pellets."

"I'll accept my apology in any of the three Bs: bucks, bacon, or bedtime extensions," Zuri said hopefully.

"Hey, Mrs. Falkenberg may be a pain, but you were out of line, too," Jessie said. "So I'm going to show you how to be the teacher's pet. Now get to bed, missy."

Zuri looked bummed. "So . . . the bacon is off the table?"

❤ ❤ ❤

Bertram stormed into the kitchen. A horrible racket had woken him from a sound sleep and he was not happy about it—especially because in his dream, he was on an island without children. He was even less happy when he saw that his kitchen was a mess.

"Enough, Mrs. Kipling, I am sick of your moody behavior!" Ravi yelled from beside the fridge.

Mrs. Kipling glared at him from across the room.

"Ravi! What's going on here?" Bertram demanded. "I was deep into my pre-bedtime nap."

"It is not me," Ravi huffed. "Talk to the irascible reptile!"

Mrs. Kipling hissed and then hurled a mug at Ravi with her tail. He ducked and the mug shattered against the wall next to Bertram.

"My 'World's Best Butler' mug!" Bertram wailed. He dropped to the ground and gathered the pieces. "I had to buy it for myself, but that doesn't make it any less precious! What are you fighting about?"

"I merely suggested Mrs. Kipling cut back on the crickets to lose the baby weight, and suddenly, she came down on me like a Mumbai monsoon!" Ravi said.

Mrs. Kipling hissed at Ravi, clearly offended, and slithered out of the kitchen.

Bertram shook his head. "I've never seen you two fight. I thought you were best friends."

"We used to be," Ravi said sadly, "but twelve kids take a toll on a relationship."

"Even four kids is enough to make you want to end it all," Bertram agreed.

"Ever since the babies left, Mrs. Kipling has been so moody and snappish. We need a break. I am going someplace where I know I will feel truly welcome. . . ." And with that, Ravi marched out of the kitchen and headed up the back stairs.

Bertram looked after him longingly. "Take me with you!"

❤ ❤ ❤

Ravi wheeled his suitcase down the hall and stopped in front of Luke's open door. He had packed all the essentials and was ready to move in with his older brother. He knew Luke would be just thrilled to share a room with him.

"Hello, roomie!" Ravi exclaimed, knocking on the doorframe.

Luke opened the door, took one look at Ravi and his suitcase, and slammed the door in Ravi's face. Ravi took a deep breath, pushed the door open, and walked in.

Luke's room was a mess. There were clothes strewn all over the floor and piled on Luke's trampoline bed, stacks of moldy old dishes, and enough crumpled paper to write ten term papers.

"Hey, Brother, I am moving in!" Ravi announced, looking around for a clean spot so he could set down his suitcase.

"If the lizard smell has finally gotten to you, you've chosen the wrong room for fresh air," Luke said, laughing as he noticed Ravi's discomfort with the mess.

"It is not the cage that stinks, it is Mrs. Kipling's attitude. I can no longer share a room with her. Luke, please do for me this solid," Ravi begged.

Luke hesitated. "Ravi, I'd love to have you here, but—"

"Great, I would love to have me here, too!" Ravi interrupted. He gave his brother a huge hug and then looked at Luke's trampoline bed. "Thank you, bro. I assume the standard 'no jumping on the bed' rule does not apply in here?"

Luke jumped onto the bed, bounced high, and did a flip in midair. "Nope! This is a rule-free zone," he said.

"Although clearly not a germ-free zone," Ravi countered. He reached down and picked up a slice of moldy cake with a melted candle sticking out of it.

"Hey! I remember that birthday!" Luke

exclaimed. He grabbed the cake from Ravi and took a big bite. "Huh, it's a little dry. . . ."

"And fuzzy," Ravi said, trying not to gag. "If you let me stay, perhaps I can turn that cake into an A-plus science project for you!"

Luke shrugged and tossed the cake over his shoulder. "Snooze. What else do I get?"

"The infinite joy of helping your brother?" Ravi said hopefully. "The time to bond and find the elusive camaraderie we have both been seeking?"

Luke simply stared at him.

Ravi sighed. "Am I correct to assume you want money?"

"Bingo," Luke said with a smile. He wrote a number down on a piece of paper and handed it to Ravi to read.

"A 'gazillion' is not a real number," Ravi said.

Just then, Emma barged in, looking frantic.

"Doesn't anybody knock anymore?" Luke said.

"Sorry, but Mrs. Kipling is in my closet, cuddling my faux-lizard pumps," Emma wailed. "Ravi, you have to come get her!"

"No. I am giving her her space," Ravi said.

"No, you're giving her *my* space," Emma said, correcting him. "And I don't want to share."

"Please, Sister!" Ravi exclaimed. He turned her around and pushed her out of the room. "I need some dude time with my bro, doing dudely bro things." Once she was in the hall, he closed the door and turned to Luke. "Now, Luke, let us color-coordinate your closet."

Dear Diary,

Ravi and Mrs. Kipling are on the outs, to put it mildly. Ravi has moved in with Luke, and Mrs. Kipling won't leave Emma alone. Unfortunately for them, I'm too busy volunteering with Zuri's class to help them sort this one out. They'll just have to handle it on their own. I'm actually looking forward to watching this mess unfold from the sidelines. It should be funny! As for Mrs. Falkenberg, matters are a bit more serious. . . .

Jessie

Chapter 3

Jessie and Zuri made sure to arrive a little early to school the next day, since they had a gift for Mrs. Falkenberg. They walked into Zuri's class together and Zuri placed a large basket of apples on Mrs. Falkenberg's desk.

"Good morning, Mrs. Falkenberg," Zuri said slowly and sweetly.

"What's all this?" Mrs. Falkenberg asked curtly, looking suspicious.

"I thought you deserved something as sweet as you are! And speaking of sah-weeeeet, way to rock that pantsuit," Zuri replied with her million-watt smile.

"Thank you," Mrs. Falkenberg said, smoothing down her outfit. "I got it when I bid on a storage locker."

Zuri gave Jessie a thumbs-up and then headed to her seat while Jessie began passing out papers. Mrs. Falkenberg sat on her desk chair, causing it to make a fart-like sound again. Zuri started to giggle, but Jessie silenced her with a sharp, stern look.

Pleasantly surprised by the lack of laughter, Mrs. Falkenberg pointed to the map. "Okay, everyone, what do we see here? Anyone?" The room remained silent. "I see Paris, I see France. Zuri, what do you see?"

Zuri turned and gave Jessie a pleading look. She wanted to laugh so badly that she felt like she was about to explode.

Jessie shook her head and hissed at Zuri, "So help me, you do not see anyone's underpants!"

Zuri sighed. "I see . . . a country known for its Gothic architecture, haute cuisine, and modernist philosophy," she replied. "And a vision of loveliness standing next to it."

Jessie smiled approvingly, but Mrs. Falkenberg was suspicious of Zuri's sudden good behavior. "Zuri, I don't know what you're trying to pull, but it's not going to work."

"*Excusez-moi?*" Zuri replied. "I am just eager to learn. *Oui, oui?*"

"Toilet talk?" Mrs. Falkenberg snapped. "That's it. Go to the corner!"

Jessie jumped to her feet. "Wait, that's not fair. She was speaking French, not making toilet talk. Zuri's been a perfect angel today!"

Mrs. Falkenberg turned and glared at Jessie.

"Oh, now it's *you* who's being disruptive. Jessie Prescott, you're on the Naughty Board."

"I've never had my name on the Naughty Board!" Jessie said, looking stunned. "All my teachers loved me!"

"Then you must have been homeschooled," Mrs. Falkenberg countered nastily. "You! Corner! Now!"

"But nobody puts Jessie in the corner!" Jessie replied, her bottom lip trembling.

Mrs. Falkenberg just shook her head and pointed to the corner.

"Except you," Jessie said, defeated. She dragged her chair into the corner. It made a fart-like noise as she pulled it. The whole class laughed. "Oh! It's just the chair, people! Stop acting like a bunch of third graders," Jessie snapped. Then she sighed. "Oh, right, you are third graders."

♥ ♥ ♥

Luke's room was finally pristine after Ravi had cleaned and sorted all day. The room was practically unrecognizable. Ravi had rolled out his yoga mat and was relaxing into the downward-facing-dog pose when Luke walked in and did a double take.

"Whoa, what did you do to my room?" Luke exclaimed.

"I merely picked up and folded your clothes to ensure they maintain a sharp crease," Ravi replied.

"So where's my purple T-shirt?" Luke asked. "It's always on the floor near the hamper."

"Second shelf on the right, with the other similarly colored tees."

Luke walked to the closet and looked at the shelf. "It's not here."

"Oh, is it a pocket tee?" Ravi asked.

"What? I don't know. Maybe," Luke said, starting to get frustrated.

"Then it is on the fourth shelf to the left with the pocket tees of like color," Ravi said. "Obviously."

"Just leave my stuff alone, okay, Ravi?" Luke huffed. "I have a system." He pulled off his dirty shirt, threw it at Ravi's head, and put on a clean one.

"Yes, I see," Ravi said, pulling the dirty shirt off his head and placing it in the hamper. Then he picked up his incense holder and waved it around the room, spreading the calming scent of sage and lavender.

"Now what are you doing?" Luke asked.

"Burning sage rids the room of negative energy . . . and hopefully that lingering armpit smell," Ravi explained. "Now I can meditate."

"Oh, goody," Luke said sarcastically. He waved

the smoke away from his face, picked up a comic book, and plopped down on his bed to read.

"Om . . . Om . . ." Ravi chanted.

"Um . . . do you mind? I'm trying to read pictures!" Luke sighed. "Can't you just make up with Mrs. Kipling?"

"Nooooooo . . . Nooooooo . . ." Ravi chanted back at him.

Luke scowled. "Oh, great, now I lost my place!"

Meanwhile, Emma and Mrs. Kipling were enjoying some quality girl time on the terrace. They were wearing matching spa robes and lounging with cucumber slices over their eyes.

"Now, see, Mrs. K, isn't this more fun than hanging out with my shoes?" Emma asked, pulling the cucumbers off of her eyes. "What am I saying? Nothing is more fun than hanging out with shoes!"

Mrs. Kipling hissed in agreement as Emma inspected her freshly pedicured toes.

"I know!" Emma exclaimed. "This pink nail color is supes cute! I'd lend it to you, but that would be crazy. You know, because you're an autumn." She stood up and gathered her things. "Well, I really should go do some homework."

Mrs. Kipling's tail lashed out and grabbed Emma around the waist.

"Ooh, you're right! An animal-print belt would look great with this robe. Okay, I guess we can go shopping again. But only if you promise not to eat any more mannequins," Emma said sternly.

Dear Diary,

Well, Operation Teacher's Pet didn't work out so well. Mrs. Falkenberg just thought Zuri was being sarcastic when she was actually being sweet. So it's on to plan B—make Mrs. Falkenberg like me. If—I mean, *when*—she realizes how great I am, maybe she'll leave Zuri alone. I call it Project Falkenfriend. Wish me luck! Not that I'll need it. She'll adore me just like all my teachers have! How could she not? Right? Right . . . ? Okay, wish me luck.

Jessie

Chapter 4

It had been another long day for Jessie and Zuri at school, and it was only noon.

"And your science project will be to prove that the Little Engine actually *couldn't*," Mrs. Falkenberg said as the bell rang. "Time for lunch!"

Jessie watched as all the kids grabbed their lunch boxes and headed out to the cafeteria. Zuri hung back and pulled Jessie aside.

"Run! Save yourself!" Zuri hissed.

"No! I'm going to make her like me or die trying," Jessie insisted.

"Now that you mention it," Zuri mused on her way to the door, "nobody knows what happened to the last teacher's aide. Oh, well." And with that, she ducked out.

"Hello," Mrs. Falkenberg said. "Did you finish your sentences?"

"Yes. I wrote 'Teachers' aides should be seen and not heard' five hundred times," Jessie answered. She handed her notebook to Mrs. Falkenberg and then rubbed her sore writing hand.

Mrs. Falkenberg flipped through the pages and raised her eyebrow critically. "Even my third graders know how to make a cursive 'B.'"

"So no smiley-face sticker?" Jessie asked hopefully.

"You have to earn those, missy."

Jessie's face fell. She looked around the classroom, desperate for something she could do to make Mrs. Falkenberg like her. Inspired, she ran to the corner and grabbed a broom and dustpan that were leaning against the wall. "Hey, why don't I sweep your classroom?"

"Put that down!" Mrs. Falkenberg exclaimed frantically. "That's not a broom, it's my trusty Firebolt!"

Jessie laughed. "And this is my Dustpan of Doom!" At the stern look on Mrs. Falkenberg's face, Jessie quit laughing. "Sorry, I don't know what we're talking about."

"I play Muggle Quidditch," Mrs. Falkenberg explained.

"Oh, a Firebolt!" Jessie said, improvising. She was still very much confused. "Right, right . . . Sorry, it's been a while since I hopped on one of *these* bad boys!"

"You play?" Mrs. Falkenberg asked hopefully.

"Uh, yeah! Didn't Zuri tell you that I love Quib—what you just said?"

"No! I used to be on an official team, but everyone's leaving to play Vampire Baseball. Don't you hate it when people don't stay loyal to their young-adult fantasy-sports genre?" Mrs. Falkenberg seemed to be really warming up to Jessie.

"Uh, it's only my number one pet peeve!" Jessie agreed enthusiastically.

"To tell you the truth, ever since the Long Island Longbottoms disbanded, I've been in a bit of a bad mood," Mrs. Falkenberg admitted.

"Really? I don't think anyone noticed," Jessie fibbed.

"Hey, wanna play Quidditch in the park this weekend?" Mrs. Falkenberg asked brightly.

"Aw, man, I would love to, but I have all these sentences to rewrite. Sigh."

"Oh, forget those!" Mrs. Falkenberg laughed. "I'll see you Saturday. Last one there is a blatching Slytherin!"

Jessie grinned. "Then I'd better leave now!"

❤ ❤ ❤

Emma was exhausted. She and Mrs. Kipling had spent the entire afternoon shopping, and Emma was desperately craving some alone time.

"Mrs. Kipling, you've got to stop being so clingy. Chunky anklets are so not in right now," Emma said as she dragged Mrs. Kipling into the apartment and uncoiled the lizard's tail from around her ankle.

Mrs. Kipling hissed.

"No, I'm not saying you're chunky! You're just . . . big-scaled," Emma said placatingly.

Mrs. Kipling hissed again, sounding angry.

"But you have a great personality!" Emma added.

Mrs. Kipling hissed louder. Her tail lashed out, barely missing Emma.

"Hey, watch it, tubby!" Emma snapped.

Mrs. Kipling lunged at her, forcing Emma to bolt for the safety of the kitchen.

Emma entered the kitchen just as Luke was in the middle of complaining to Bertram. "So you gotta help me get Ravi out of my room! He won't stop cleaning!"

"Give him a few years," Bertram answered. "He'll give up, like I did."

"Mrs. Kipling is driving me crazy!" Emma announced. "I had to spend all day with her in the makeup department, and it's official: there's no way to match her scale tone!"

"We have to find a way to get those two crazy kids back together, before Ravi makes me look at paint swatches. I don't even know what a swatch is, and I'd like to keep it that way," Luke insisted.

"Agreed," Emma said, looking beseechingly at Bertram. "I can't handle trying on any more faux-lizard-skin accessories. A girl only needs so much of the same print!"

"Fine," Bertram said with a sigh. "But what's in it for me?"

Luke handed him a piece of paper with a number written on it.

"A 'gazillion' is not a real number," Bertram said.

❤ ❤ ❤

Later that night, Jessie found Zuri coloring happily in the living room. It was the first time Jessie had seen her so cheerful in days.

"I don't know what you said to Mrs. Falkenberg, but she was in the best mood all afternoon," Zuri told Jessie with a huge grin. "Our only homework is to watch TV! Which, ironically, makes me not want to do it."

"She's been texting me a lot. I wanted to make her like me, but I think I may have overdone it," Jessie said, scrunching up her nose as she looked at her phone, which buzzed with a new text.

"Don't worry. Even if she is an extreme clinger, it's not like she knows where we live," Zuri said, trying to reassure her.

Just then, the elevator doors slid open and Mrs. Falkenberg stepped out, carrying several large scrolls. "Yooo-hooo! Jessie! I found you!" Mrs. Falkenberg called out in a singsong voice.

"Mrs. Falkenberg?" Jessie asked. "How did you get our address?"

"Confidential school records, silly!" Mrs. Falkenberg said with a laugh.

"Apparently not so confidential," Jessie muttered.

"I thought we could go over some team plays, so we can dive right in at Quidditch practice tomorrow," Mrs. Falkenberg continued. Then she turned to Zuri. "And why aren't you watching TV?"

"Oh, all right," Zuri huffed. She walked into the screening room, leaving Jessie alone with Mrs. Falkenberg.

Mrs. Falkenberg sat down on the couch and unrolled the scrolls she had, revealing complicated diagrams of Quidditch plays. They were covered with x's and o's and lightning bolts. The whole thing made Jessie's head spin.

"O-kay. Mrs. Falkenberg—" Jessie said.

"Please, call me by my Quidditch name: Madame McSniggles," Mrs. Falkenberg interrupted, putting her hands on her hips and grinning.

"Yeah, Mrs. Falkenberg, this really isn't a good time. . . ." Jessie tried again. "We're about to have dinner and then I need to put the kids to bed. . . ."

"Oh. I'm sorry. I'm just so glad I finally found a friend who gets me!" Mrs. Falkenberg explained excitedly. "Hey! Want to grab dinner before practice tomorrow?"

"I'd love to, but . . . I don't like to eat before a big game," Jessie said, clearly groping for an excuse.

"You're right." Mrs. Falkenberg shook her head. "Silly me! We'll go after. See you tomorrow, bestie!" She headed to the elevator, leaving the scrolls behind. "And don't forget to study those plays tonight."

"Try and stop me!" Jessie called after her as the elevator doors closed. Zuri immediately ran back in from the screening room.

"This is working out *great!*" Zuri exclaimed.

"Yeah, for *you!*" Jessie groaned, flopping down onto the couch. "But Mrs. Falkenberg and I don't have anything in common."

"You have *me* in common," Zuri said matter-of-factly. "And if you want me to keep being a star student, you're going to jump on that broom tomorrow and work it like a pure-blood!"

Dear Diary,

How did I get myself into such a mess? I wanted Mrs. Falkenberg to like me—not to be my new best friend forever. I don't mind making a new friend (even if she is a little odd), but if I start playing Muggle Quidditch in Central Park, I'm pretty sure she'll be my *only* friend before too long! Time to think of plan C. But first I need to reread those Harry Potter books, because I know nothing about Quidditch and these plays are making my eye twitch. Speaking of a Twitch, isn't that the golden flying thing with the little wings?

Jessie

Chapter 5

The next morning, Jessie put on the Quidditch uniform that Mrs. Falkenberg had left for her, and she reluctantly made her way to an empty field in Central Park. Mrs. Falkenberg was waiting for her, wearing a lime-green jersey, soccer shorts, knee-high socks, and cleats. She carried two brooms, had set up six hoops on posts—three on each end of the field—and had laid out three balls on the ground.

"Hey there, bestie!" Mrs. Falkenberg called cheerfully as soon as she spotted Jessie.

"Hey," Jessie said with noticeably less enthusiasm. "Quick question. Why does the back of my jersey say 'Furtenfurter'?"

"Didn't you say that was your Quidditch name?"

"No, that was a sneeze," Jessie explained. Then she looked around. "Hey, where are your other friends?"

"What other friends?" Mrs. Falkenberg replied seriously.

"Oh," Jessie replied awkwardly. She had assumed they would be playing with a few people, and she definitely hadn't realized that she was now Mrs. Falkenberg's only friend.

Mrs. Falkenberg handed Jessie a scruffy-looking old broom. "Here. Sorry, you have to practice with my old Cleansweep Eleven. Maybe one day you'll work your way up to one of these babies!" She held out her Firebolt broom.

"A girl can dream," Jessie said sarcastically, although the sarcasm seemed to be lost on Mrs. Falkenberg.

"Now, remember the rules: no blagging, blatching, blurting, haversacking, or Quaffle-pocking. Obviously, we don't have to worry about Snitch-nipping or stooging," Mrs. Falkenberg told her.

"Obviously," Jessie said. "But if you could just refresh my—"

"Brooms up!" Mrs. Falkenberg interrupted. Then she mounted her broom, scooped up a ball from the ground, and chucked it at Jessie, knocking Jessie to the ground.

"Ow! Foul!" Jessie shrieked. "I'm pretty sure I've just been blag-boozled or something!"

"It was not a foul!" Mrs. Falkenberg insisted. "Beaters throw Bludgers at Chasers to make them drop Quaffles. Duh! That's only Quidditch 101!"

"Can we switch to Quidditch 911?" Jessie groaned. "I think I broke my furtenfurter."

"You seem a little rusty. Why don't you try playing the Golden Snitch?" Mrs. Falkenberg suggested.

"Does it mean I get to change clothes?" Jessie asked hopefully, pulling at her embarrassing Quidditch jersey.

"What kind of Snitch would you be if you didn't?" Mrs. Falkenberg replied.

❤ ❤ ❤

Twenty minutes later, Jessie was back on the field, but this time she was dressed head to toe in a tightly fitting gold spandex outfit—gold leggings, a gold dress, and a short gold cape—and a shiny gold sock with a tennis ball inside it was tucked into Jessie's waistband, like a tail.

Mrs. Falkenberg pulled out a crown with wings and placed it on Jessie's head.

"Well, this makes the whole thing work—" Jessie said sarcastically.

"Brooms up!" Mrs. Falkenberg barked, interrupting Jessie yet again. Then she tackled Jessie to the ground and grabbed the sock from Jessie's waistband. She hopped up and waved the sock over her head. "I've snatched the Snitch! Eat my bristles!"

"Can I go back to being a Chaser?" Jessie moaned from the ground.

❤ ❤ ❤

"Gold star, gold star, kitty sticker . . . Man, I am cleaning up!" Zuri said happily to herself as she flipped through her graded homework from the week. She was lounging on the couch, enjoying her weekend for the first time since she started third grade. The elevator door opened and Jessie limped into the living room. Jessie was still in her Snitch outfit, but it was torn and dirty. "Whoa! You look like a banana from the bottom of someone's backpack!" Zuri exclaimed.

"I can't believe they let children play Quidditch. Is Professor Dumbledore aware of how dangerous it is?" Jessie asked as she collapsed onto the couch.

"You just have to last until June. Hopefully my fourth-grade teacher will be into something safer, like cliff diving," Zuri said reassuringly.

"Zuri, sweetie," Jessie said gently. "I can't keep being Mrs. Falkenberg's friend."

"What? Why not?"

"Maybe because she makes me ride a broom in public and yell things like 'For the glory of Hufflepuff!'" Jessie clenched her fist as she said it.

"But, Jessie," Zuri pleaded, "you saw what she was like before! If you break up with her, I'll have to go back to slumming it in the corner, which is really close to Gassy Gus! What is that kid eating?"

Jessie shook her head. "I just feel bad for lying to Mrs. Falkenberg. She's actually a nice person, and she deserves a real best friend who genuinely shares her interests."

"Yeah, yeah," Zuri said, wrinkling her nose. "Can't you just learn to like Quidditch?"

"Can't you just learn to like vegetables?" Jessie countered.

Zuri gulped. "I see your point."

❤ ❤ ❤

Ravi rushed into Luke's room, waving his phone wildly. "I got your text, roomie," he called. "Did you not understand the vacuuming schedule?"

"Now!" Luke yelled from his bed, where he was lounging.

Bertram jumped out from behind Luke's door

and shut it, blocking the door with his body. Then Emma came out of the bathroom, dragging a reluctant Mrs. Kipling along on a leash.

"Come on!" Emma said, tugging on the leash. "Get out here!"

"What are you people doing?" Ravi asked, shaking his head firmly. "I told you, Mrs. Kipling and I are not speaking!"

"Well, you're not leaving this room until you talk through your problems," Bertram said.

Mrs. Kipling hissed angrily.

"There is nothing to talk about. Mrs. Kipling and I have just grown apart," Ravi said sadly. "It is over."

Emma and Luke exchanged looks. They knew just how to play it.

"Well, maybe you dodged a bullet, Ravi," Emma said, putting her arm around her brother and lowering her voice. "Mrs. Kipling *is* pretty needy and clingy."

"Yeah, I don't know how you put up with her for so long," Luke agreed.

"Me neither. It's always *all* about her: 'I need a walk.' 'I want my claws filed.' 'I ordered this rat medium rare!' She is a terrible friend!" Emma added.

"Now just hold on a moment," Ravi said, clearly getting upset. "Mrs. K has not been a bad friend. She has just been a little . . . down in the swamps lately."

"A little?" Emma scoffed. "I asked her to quit being such a diva, and she almost bit my head off—literally!"

"Yeah, you don't need to defend her, Ravi. We're on your side, bro." Luke nodded. "Lizards be crazy."

"Enough!" Ravi shouted, stomping his foot.

"Mrs. Kipling is the most loyal, funny, supportive best friend there has ever been! I can't believe you would say such awful things about her! Come on, Mrs. K, we are going home!"

Bertram opened the door, and Ravi and Mrs. Kipling marched out of Luke's room. As soon as the door closed, Emma, Bertram, and Luke all high-fived each other.

"It worked!" Emma squealed. "Bertram, you actually had a good idea!"

"And after that rutabaga casserole, you really needed a win," Luke said.

"Hey, I felt appreciated for almost five seconds. Thanks for that," Bertram said sarcastically.

Just then, Ravi pushed open the door. "BTW, Mrs. Kipling and I just figured out what happened in here," he said sternly. Then he smiled. "And we love you for it!"

Dear Diary,

I know I'm going to have to let Mrs. Falkenberg down, but I can't think of a good way to do it. I was planning on telling her that I'm allergic to grassy fields. Then I thought of taking it one step further and explaining to her that I'm allergic to Quidditch. But I fear she'll see right through me no matter how I try to spin it. I just can't be her friend anymore. I hope she doesn't get upset—for my sake and for Zuri's. It's just that she deserves a real best friend who also likes Quidditch. A girl like me can only be blag-boozled for so long!

Jessie

Chapter 6

All through the night, Jessie was dreading playing Quidditch with Mrs. Falkenberg. The next day, she waited outside her classroom until the bell rang. She was wearing her patched-up Quidditch uniform and was dragging a mop. From the hallway, she could hear Mrs. Falkenberg, who sounded happy. Jessie just couldn't crush her spirit.

"Quitting time!" Mrs. Falkenberg announced. "Do your homework if you feel like it! No pressure!"

The kids all gathered up their things and left just as Jessie walked in.

"I'm ready for practice," Jessie announced in a monotone voice. She held up her mop. "Since I broke your Cleansweep Eleven, I hope it's okay that I brought this . . . Schmutz Buster Five-Thousand?"

"Yeah, about that . . ." Mrs. Falkenberg said delicately. "Jessie, you don't need to come to practice today."

"Why? Is my broom grip not as bad as we thought?" Jessie asked, looking amazed.

"No, no, it is. But . . . and this is awkward . . . I'm going to practice with Mr. Itzel instead," Mrs. Falkenberg explained.

"Mr. Itzel?" Jessie asked. "The librarian?"

"Yes! Can you believe he was a Beater for the Central Park Centaurs? How hot is that?" Mrs. Falkenberg gushed.

"I'm tingling, but—" Jessie began.

"No offense, Jessie, but you're a *rotten* Chaser, a *horrible* Keeper, and you seem a few Horcruxes short of a soul, if you know what I mean," Mrs. Falkenberg interrupted.

"I do not!" Jessie snapped, looking offended. "And I thought I was a really good Snootch!"

Just then, a fair-skinned man, Mr. Itzel, appeared, dressed in his Quidditch uniform. He was wearing round Harry Potter–style glasses and carrying a Firebolt broom. He smiled and waved happily at Mrs. Falkenberg from the doorway. Mrs. Falkenberg took Jessie by the shoulders and shook her gently. "Jessie, don't be upset. It's not me. It's you." She picked up her broom and grabbed Mr. Itzel's hand. "Let's go, stud muffin."

Jessie watched in awe as the pair left, and then she plopped down in Mrs. Falkenberg's desk chair.

It made a fart-like noise. "Oh, shut up!" Jessie snapped at it.

Zuri walked in a moment later. "I just saw Mrs. Falkenberg and Mr. Itzel heading into the park. I guess you're off the hook."

"I can't believe Mrs. Falkenberg dumped me for someone who sunburns in fluorescent lighting."

"I can," Zuri said matter-of-factly. "I set them up."

"You did?" Jessie asked. "Why?"

"Well, I thought about how you said Mrs. F deserved a real best friend. And when I saw how unhappy Ravi was without *his* best friend, I knew I had to find Mrs. Falkenberg *her* Mrs. Kipling," Zuri explained.

"Aw, but how did you know Mr. Itzel would be a perfect match?" Jessie smiled. She was touched by Zuri's thoughtfulness.

"He wears little round glasses, an owl sweater, and calls his minivan the Hogwarts Express." Zuri shrugged. "I took a wild guess."

Jessie pulled Zuri into a big hug. "Well, that was very sweet of you, Zuri."

"You're not really upset that you got dumped, are you?" Zuri asked.

"Nah. At least this breakup didn't involve my birthday and a jumbotron. But she'll miss me." Jessie flipped back her cape. "They always miss me."

Luke walked into his room to find that it looked like a tornado had swept through it. There were clothes everywhere, papers scattered all over the floor, and piles of dirty dishes on every available surface.

"What happened in here?" he yelled.

Ravi and Mrs. Kipling jumped out from behind his bed. "Surprise!" Ravi yelled. "I wanted to thank you for letting me crash at your bachelor pad."

"So let me get this straight," Luke said. "You and Mrs. Kipling waited for me to leave the apartment, then you came in here and trashed my room . . . to *thank* me?"

"That is correct," Ravi said, nodding.

"Dude," Luke exclaimed, "you are the best brother ever!"

Luke pulled Ravi into a big hug and then high-fived Mrs. Kipling's tail.

"I know, right? Maybe the three of us should room together!" Ravi suggested enthusiastically.

Luke's smile faded and he glared at Ravi, pointing at the door. "Get out."

Dear Diary,

Zuri did the sweetest thing! I know, I almost didn't believe it myself, but she really saved the day! She spared me from the potentially awkward situation of having to fake a friendship or, worse, having to end one! I owe that kid big-time! Ravi and Mrs. Kipling are friends again, and Luke has his room back to himself. Basically, everything is great. I may be lousy at Quidditch and at letting people down, but I'm pretty magical when it comes to these kids! We're like one big happy wizard clan! Wait, is that even an actual thing? (Okay, I seriously need to reread those books.)

Jessie